Back on the Farm

by Jehu David McJunkin & Amelia A. Wethern

NOSTALGIC SCENARIOS OF YESTERYEAR ON THE FARM

OTHER BOOK BY JEHU DAVID MCJUNKIN

A Missouri River Tale

ISBN-13: 978-0-9766124-1-4

ISBN-10: 0-9766124-1-0

Co-Author and Published by Amelia A. Wethern

BJ	Part Colorist
Ben Nugent	Cover Designer
Mary Ann Lyles	Web Designer
Ariel M. Wethern	Typeset & Proof Reader
Ashley M. Fulks	Typeset & Proof Reader
Tirzah A. Wethern	Consultant
Arlene K. Wethern	Consultant

Ãþ Amelia Press

P.O Box 303

Moorhead, MN 56560-0303

www.davidmcjunkin.com

Printed in the United States of America

Howdy Folks !

Crunch on the farm

Acknowledgements

Special thanks to these following people that made this book possible.

My parents Edith and John McJunkin for always bringing home a roll of white butcher paper and pencils for me to draw

My late wife Marty who was very supportive of my drawings and writing while we were married for 52 years

My sisters Margaret E. Youker & Jean Eggleston for always encouraging me in my drawings

My second wife Anita for believing and supporting me in publishing my book

The Wethern Girls for playing the violin and piano

Mary McJunkin Ochsner

Arlene A. Banares

Mary Ann Lyles

***

"WHAT ARE YOU DOING WITH MY KITCHEN BROOM AND DUSTPAN, I HOPE YOU DIDN'T USE IT CLEANING THE BARN?"

"MARTY, THOSE THRESHERS LICKED THEIR PLATES SO CLEAN THERE'S NOT A THING LEFT FOR THE DOGS."

"I KNOW YOU CAUGHT TWO BIG ONES, BUT GET THEM OUT OF THIS HOUSE IMMEDIATELY!"

"FOLKS, IT'S SO NICE TO SELL COWBOYS HATS TO TWO NICE PEOPLE WHO ACTUALLY TEND COWS."

"DAVE, I'VE NEVER SEEN SUCH BEAUTIFUL PLANTS, SO TALL AND STATELY WITH TASSELS WAVING ON TOP, MUST BE A BIG CROP OF SOYBEANS OR TOMATOES."

"ALICE, WE'LL HAVE TO SEE HOW STRENUOUS THIS ICE FISHING REALLY IS."

"THE OLSONS MUST BE GOING TO BED. I SEE THEIR UPSTAIRS LIGHT GO ON."

"I GUESS WE HAVE TO USE THE WAGON TODAY, I DON'T HAVE ENOUGH GAS TO MAKE IT TO TOWN THEM OLSON BOYS BEEN SIPHONING THE TANK AGAIN."

"I KNOW THE HORSES KNOW THE WAY HOME, BUT DO THEY KNOW ENOUGH TO STOP AT THE RAILROAD TRACK?"

"AN ORPHANED DEER IS OUT THERE. I FEEL SO SORRY FOR HIM. I FEEL BAD NOW THAT I COOKED THAT VENISON STEAK."

"OUR NEW NEIGHBOR FROM THE CITY ASKED IF THERE WERE ANY STORES IN TOWN THAT HANDLED SHOES FOR HORSES."

"LOOK AT THE HIGH SNOW DRIFTS IN THE BULL PEN, I THOUGHT THE WEATHERMAN SAID ON THE RADIO LAST NIGHT THAT WE'RE ONLY GETTING A COUPLE INCHES OF SNOW."

"FIDDLE DEE DEE THE FLY HAS MARRIED THE BUMBLE BEE. MOTHER WAS RIGHT, I SPEND MY TIME SCRUBBING INSTEAD OF SHOPPING."

"DAVE, I FEEL GUILTY ASKING GEORGE AND MABLE TO TAKE CARE OF OUR FARM WHILE WE'RE GONE. I KIND OF MISS OUR FARM, DON'T YOU?"

"MARTY, LOOK WHAT I FOUND BEHIND THE OUTHOUSE, MY OLD FAVORITE BARN BOOTS. I'VE BEEN WONDERING FOR WEEKS WHERE I LEFT THEM."

"IT'S KIND OF NICE TO GET AWAY FROM THE WOMEN FOR AWHILE, SO WE CAN HAVE A MAN TO MAN TALK."

"DAVE, DON'T TELL ME YOU WOULD SELL ONE OF OUR NICE COWS
TO BUY A LITTLE OLD FISHING BOAT."

"DAVE WAKE UP! YOU MUST CALL OUR BARN CATS IN TO TEACH THESE MICE SOME MANNERS."

"GEORGE, I THINK FATHER IS PRAYING IN THERE."

"BLESS YOUR HEART LITTLE MOTHER, YOU'VE GOT FOUR EGGS FOR ME."

"OH DAVE! WHAT ABOUT OUR POOR COWS."

"I'M SORRY TO WAKE YOU, BUT IT'S TIME FOR YOU TO FIX THE TRACTOR AGAIN."

"DAVE, THE ONE THING WE OUTHOUSE PEOPLE DON'T HAVE TO WORRY ABOUT IS HAVING PLUMBING PROBLEMS."

"GOODNESS! MY DRESS GOT UNZIPPED ZIP IT UP QUICKLY BEFORE SOMEONE SEES ME."

"MARTY, LOOK AT THE LITTLE ORPHANED PIGLET I'VE BROUGHT HOME FOR YOU TO BOTTLE FEED."

"DAVE DEAR, WHEN WE GET TO MOTHER'S DON'T WORRY HER ABOUT OUR MORTGAGE PAYMENT AND FOR HEAVEN SAKE NO DISGUSTING TALES OF COW PIES."

"MA, THE JUDGE GAVE PEGGY 1ST PLACE BECAUSE I GAVE HER A BATH AND SHE SMELLS GOOD."

"YOU MIGHT AS WELL CLEAN THE STABLES DAVE, IT'S STARTING TO RAIN AND YOU WON'T BE ABLE TO DO ANYTHING OUT IN THE FIELD TODAY."

"REMEMBER, IF WE SEE A SIX POINT BUCK, IT'S MINE TO SHOOT."

"YOU'RE NOT GETTING OUT OF BED, THE DOG IS PROBABLY ONLY BARKING AT THE MOON."

"I KNOW YOU DON'T WANT ME TO BOTHER YOU WHEN YOU ARE READING THE PAPER, BUT A BIRD JUST FLEW IN AND IS EATING YOUR EGGS."

"GOOD HEAVENS, DAVE, YOU FORGOT TO PUT ON YOUR NECKTIE !"

"YOU BETTER NOT BE BRINGING THOSE SMELLY BARN SHOES OF YOURS IN HERE."

"SIR, WE WOULD LIKE TO SEE YOUR LINE OF SECOND-HAND OLD TRACTORS."

"WHEN YOU TWO SAY MILKING IS FUN, SOMETIMES I WISH EUGENE AND I NEVER SOLD OUR FARM."

"TRY IT, YOU ALWAYS SAY THE MEAT IS AS TOUGH AS SHOE LEATHER."

"WOW! FRESH BEAR TRACKS, A MAMA AND HER CUB MUST HAVE PASSED THROUGH LAST NIGHT. I'D SURE HATE TO MEET UP WITH THEM."

"MABLE, I SEE DAVE SHOWING OFF HIS WOOD PILE, SO I'LL SHOW YOU MY CAN GOODS."

"I WONDER WHEN THE JOHNSON'S ARE COMING HOME FROM FLORIDA."

"ALICE, I UPHOSTERED MY CHAIR AND THE SOFA AND HAD ENOUGH MATERIALS LEFT OVER TO MAKE A DRESS FOR ME AND A SHIRT FOR DAVE."

"COME ON MARTY, I DON'T LIKE THE WAY THAT DRUG STORE COWBOY IS LOOKING AT YOU."

"DAVE, IS THAT YOU AND CRUNCH ?; I BET YOU BOYS ARE REALLY HUNGRY AND READY FOR SUPPER."

"CLARA, I WANT TO GET OUT OF HERE BEFORE DAVE DECIDES HE WANTS ME TO HELP HIM SHOVEL OUT THE PIG HOUSE."

"MARTY, WILL YOU MILK THE COWS TOMORROW? GEORGE AND I ARE GOING FISHING FOR WALLEYE AT BIG CORMORANT LAKE."

"MR. OLSON IS SELLING FIVE OF HIS HEIFER COWS, CAN YOU HANDLE MILKING FIVE MORE, MARTY?"

"DAVE, I'D RATHER BE RIDING A HORSE THAN CLEANING THE STABLES."

"MARTY, I HOPE YOU BROUGHT SOME MONEY."

"I'M JUST LOOKING AT THE SEARS CATALOG. YOU DON'T HAVE
TO LOOK SO WORRIED, BESIDES I CAN'T WEAR THESE FASHIONS
IN TOWN. FOLKS MIGHT THINK WE HAVE MONEY."

"DAVE IS HAVING HIS PICTURE TAKEN WITH ROSA. SHE GOT A RIBBON AT THE COUNTY FAIR. NOW, DAVE BRAGS ABOUT HER EVERYWHERE WE GO."

"DAVE, WE CERTAINLY HAVE A LOT OF MOUTHS TO FEED."

"WAKE UP DAVE, BULL PHONED. HE SAID YOU'D BETTER GET DOWN TO THE BARN AND MILK HIS COWS."

"MARTY,. WE'RE ONLY STAYING FOR THE WEEKEND AT YOUR MOTHER'S PLACE NOT A WHOLE WEEK."

"DAVE, I HOPE YOU REMEMBER TO BRING THE WORMS, BECAUSE I DIDN'T."

"MARTY, SINCE WE INSTALLED THAT STEREO SPEAKER, THERE ARE TIMES I FEEL THE COWS ARE BREATHING TO THE BEAT OF THE MUSIC."

"DAVE, MABLE SAID SHE SAW A SHOW ON TV HOW SOME RICH WOMEN BATHE IN MILK TO KEEP THEIR SKIN SOFT. MAYBE I SHOULD TRY IT, WHAT DO YOU THINK?"

"DAVE, DON'T LOOK AT ME LIKE THAT, YOU WERE LISTENING WHEN I READ AUNT EDITH'S LETTER. SHE SAID HER ADDRESS WAS 1920 COMO STREET. IT'S A BEAUTIFUL HOUSE OF SOLID BRICK WITH PLENTY OF GROUNDS. YOU CAN'T MISS IT."

"I HEAR THE MEETING BELL, NOW REMEMBER IF GEORGE MAKES A FOOL OF HIMSELF, DON'T YOU."

"WHY DID YOU LET THAT HAPPEN. NOW, I'LL BE LATE SHOPPING WITH THE GIRLS IN TOWN, I HOPE YOU BROUGHT A SPARE TIRE."

"I HOPE OLD MUD RUNNER DOESN'T DECIDE TO QUIT ON US NOW."

"NOW DAVE, I KNOW YOU WOULDN'T WANT ME TO PUT ON MY PANTS AND GO OUT AND SHOVEL THAT SNOW WHILE YOU STAY INSIDE AND DO THE DISHES."

"HERE COMES SANTA CLAUS FROM THE NORTH POLE. I WONDER WHAT HE BROUGHT HIS LITTLE DUMPLING, HOPEFULLY SOME SWEETS."

"DAVE, SMILE, PRETEND YOU'RE ENJOYING YOURSELF. I KNOW YOU FEEL FUNNY BEING THE ONLY MAN AT THIS PARTY, BUT NO ONE TOLD ME IT'S THE DEER OPENER TODAY."

"I KNOW IT'S HOT OUTSIDE, BUT THIS IS THE FOURTH TIME YOU'VE COME IN FOR FOOD AND IT'S NOT EVEN LUNCH YET. WHY DON'T YOU CLEAN THE STABLES, IT'S COOLER THERE."

"MARTY, WHAT DO I SAY TO ROSA TO MAKE HER SMILE ? MY FRIENDS IN THE CITY WANT A PICTURE OF A COW SMILING."

"I'M GLAD I DON'T HAVE TO WEAR THIS STRAITJACKET AND CARDBOARD HAT TO WORK EVERYDAY. IT'S SURE NICE BEING A FARMER."

"OH DAVE IS OUT CHOPPING WOOD WITH GEORGE. I'VE GOT TO RUN, ETHEL, THEY'LL BE IN SOON FOR LUNCH. I CAN'T WAIT TO HEAR THE REST OF THE GOSSIPS YOU HEARD ON THE PARTY LINE ABOUT THE NEW NEIGHBOR, AS SOON AS THEY ARE GONE I'LL CALL YOU."

"COME ON MARTY, LOOK AT THIS PUMPKIN, OUR LITTLE ARLENE WILL LOVE IT. IT REMINDS ME OF OUR OLD UNCLE GORDON."

"YOU'RE HOME EARLY! ROSA IS IN LABOUR AT THE BARN. DOC IS ON HIS WAY. BETTER CHANGE TO YOUR OVERALLS."

"MABLE THINKS HER AND I SHOULD GO WITH YOU AND GEORGE TO THE FARMERS CONVENTION IN ST. PAUL."

"NOW, WHICH ONE OF YOU GALS WANTS TO BE MILKED FIRST."

"DAVE, ONE THING I LIKE ABOUT BEING A FARMER. YOU CAN STOP AND CHAT IF YOU FEEL LIKE IT WITHOUT SOME BOSSY FOREMAN STICKING HIS NOSE OVER YOUR SHOULDER."

"DAVE, SINCE THAT OLSON KID STARTED DRIVING I'M ALMOST AFRAID TO CROSS THE STREET FOR OUR MAIL."

" I KNOW YOU LIKE THAT SHIRT, BUT YOU WORE IT ALL THE TIME AT
THE COUNTY FAIR DANCE AND TO CHURCH THE LAST FIVE WEEKS."

"I HOPE THE ANDERSONS COME TO CHURCH. THEY MISSED TWO SUNDAYS IN A ROW."

"MARTY, THERE'S A FAMILY OF MICE LIVING IN MY DRESS SHOES."

"WELL, DAVE, THAT JUST SHOWS HOW LONG IT'S BEEN SINCE YOU TOOK ME OUT."

"WAKE UP HONEY, YOUR FRIEND IS HERE TO LET YOU KNOW IT'S MILKING TIME."

"I HOPE YOU HAVE A GOOD TIME AT THE COUNTY FAIR, YOU LOOK
LIKE A DREAM IN YOUR NEW NAPOLEON HAT."

"GEORGE CALLED TO REMIND YOU ABOUT THE FARMER'S CONVENTION TOMORROW. YOU MEN DON'T KNOW HOW LUCKY YOU ARE GOING OFF TO THE CONVENTION WHILE YOUR WIVES ARE STUCK AT HOME CLEANING THE HOUSE AND TAKING CARE OF THE FARM."

"DAVE, WHILE YOU WERE FISHING, I CALLED MABLE OVER AND HER AND I HELPED ALICE GIVE BIRTH TO HER CALF. PEGGY GAVE BIRTH TO SEVEN LITTLE PIGLETS, SO I THINK I'LL GIVE THAT FISH TO MABLE FOR HELPING."

"MY MOTHER IN LAW IS COMING FOR THE SUMMER AND MY WIFE WANTS ME TO GIVE UP MY BED AND SLEEP IN THE BARN WITH THE COWS. I SAID SHE AND HER MOTHER COULD SLEEP WITH THE COWS, SHE STARTED CRYING SO I DECIDED TO GET MY HAIR CUT."

"MA, I'M SO GLAD YOU CAME, MA. YOU AND I CAN SLEEP ON OUR BIG NEW QUEEN BED AND YOU CAN STAY AS LONG AS YOU LIKE. I KNOW DAVE DOESN'T MIND SLEEPING ON OUR COUCH OR THE BARN."

"GEORGE, MARTY IS LISTENING IN ON THE PARTY LINE. WE'D BETTER TURN DOWN THE COWBOY SHOW."

"WELL, LUCKY-DOG, I BETTER GET THIS FIRE STARTED OR WE'LL NEVER GET DAVE HIS BREAKFAST AND WE KNOW HOW HE LIKES IT ON TIME AND HOT."

"DAVE, DON'T LOOK BACK NOW BUT YOU SHOULD HAVE FIXED THE BULL PEN YESTERDAY, LIKE I TOLD YOU TO."

"DAVE, MABLE AND GEORGE ARE BUYING A MILKING MACHINE THIS YEAR. DO YOU THINK WE'LL MAKE ENOUGH MONEY TO BUY ONE TOO?"

"WELL, NOBODY CAN SAY I'M NOT FOLLOWING DOC'S ORDERS, HE SAID DRINK PLENTY OF LIQUIDS."

"DAVE, DON'T FORGET TO GIVE DOC TWO DOZEN EGGS, VENISON STEAKS, MILK AND PORK ROAST FOR COMING IN TO CHECK ON ALICE'S CALF.

"OUR NEW NEIGHBOR FROM THE CITY DROVE BY. I DON'T KNOW WHY HIS WIFE ALWAYS ASKS ME IF I'M GETTING READY TO PICK UP A BALE OF HAY."

"MARTY, I'M THINKING OF SELLING A FEW ACRES, SO WE CAN FIX THE BARN, HOUSE, TRACTOR AND BUY A NEW FISHING BOAT. WHAT DO YOU THINK ?"

"DAVE, I KNOW IT'S THE STEAM THRESHER DAY AT ROLLAG BUT WE'RE OUT OF FIREWOOD FOR THE STOVE, YOU NEED TO CHOP SOME BEFORE YOU AND GEORGE LEAVE."

"MARTY, I THINK OUR COWS WANT TO LISTEN TO THE BASEBALL GAME NOW INSTEAD OF CLASSICAL MUSIC."

"MABLE, DON'T YOU JUST LOVE THE SMELL OF THE BARN?"

"ANGEL HONEY, DOC HASN'T ASKED YOU TO PUT OUT YOUR TONGUE YET."

"OUR COW ONLY STEPPED ON MY LEFT FOOT, BUT THE HOT WATER FEELS SO GOOD I PUT BOTH IN."

I was born at seven o'clock in the morning on July 30th, 1918 in the little town of Geneva, Illinois, thirty-seven miles west of Chicago. My first grade teacher, Miss McBreen, had been teaching for forty years, and I had her the year which was to be her last year of teaching. She was very firm with her students and often slapped their hands with a ruler. The other punishment was you had to sit under her desk for a time, so I spent my free time drawing. A very good friend of mine, John Jarvis, lived across the street and we started drawing together. When my friend graduated from high school, he went to an art school and became a cartoonist.

When I was in the fifth grade, my sister got scarlet fever, and I remember the policeman came and nailed a red sign on our door saying, "Keep Out." I had been sharing a bedroom with her and came down with a slight case. I remember my father bringing home a roll of white butcher's paper, and I taped it on the wall and drew on it.

My family moved 12 miles away to Wheaton, when I was twelve years old, and I got my own bedroom. I corresponded with my friend, John Jarvis, and we sent jokes back and forth for a couple of years. I joined the cartooning club in high school, and I remember our leader took us into Chicago to the Chicago Daily News and we met Mr. Shoemacker, who was their political cartoonist. He gave each of us one of his original drawings. During those high school years, I was drawing as soon as I got home from school. My homeroom teacher allowed me to take jokes and pass them around the room. I think she thought I had talent and might be a cartoonist someday.

When I went to college, I didn't major in Art, but in English. I had an uncle who had an advertising company, and I secretly hoped to get a job there someday. However, when I graduated from college, he gave me his copy-writing test and I didn't pass.

One month after I graduated from college, I married my sweetheart of four years, Marty, we settled down in a small house in Geneva, where I had been born. We went ahead and had seven children. We were married for fifty two years. She died more than ten years ago. She was very supportive of my drawings and writing.

I bought a farm up in Northern Minnesota as a getaway place and have owned it for more than forty years. Owning the farm put me in contact with farmers. I got to see how they lived and what they did for recreation and what they think about. So, I decided to write cartoons, which I titled "Back on the Farm."

I have spent a good number of hours drawing over the past 25 years. I retired and wrote three books about sheep who could walk on their hind hooves and talk like humans. I divided my time between writing and drawing.

I hope you will find pleasure reading my book.

Sincerely yours,

Jehu David McJunkin